On Our Vacation

ANNE ROCKWELL

E. P. DUTTON · NEW YORK

for Oliver Penn and Henry

Published in the United States by
E. P. Dutton, New York, N.Y.,
a division of NAL Penguin Inc.

Published simultaneously in Canada by
Fitzhenry & Whiteside Limited, Toronto

Library of Congress Cataloging-in-Publication Data
Rockwell, Anne F.
  On our vacation/Anne Rockwell.—1st ed.
        p.   cm.
  Summary: Throughout the Bear Family's summer vacation,
objects and activities related to the setting are displayed
for preschoolers' identification.
  ISBN 0-525-44487-4
  [1. Vacations—Fiction.   2. Camping—Fiction.
3. Islands—Fiction.]   I. Title.   88-29996
PZ7.R5943On   1989   CIP
[E]—dc19   AC

We are going on vacation tomorrow—
my mother, my father and me!

These are the things we pack in our car.

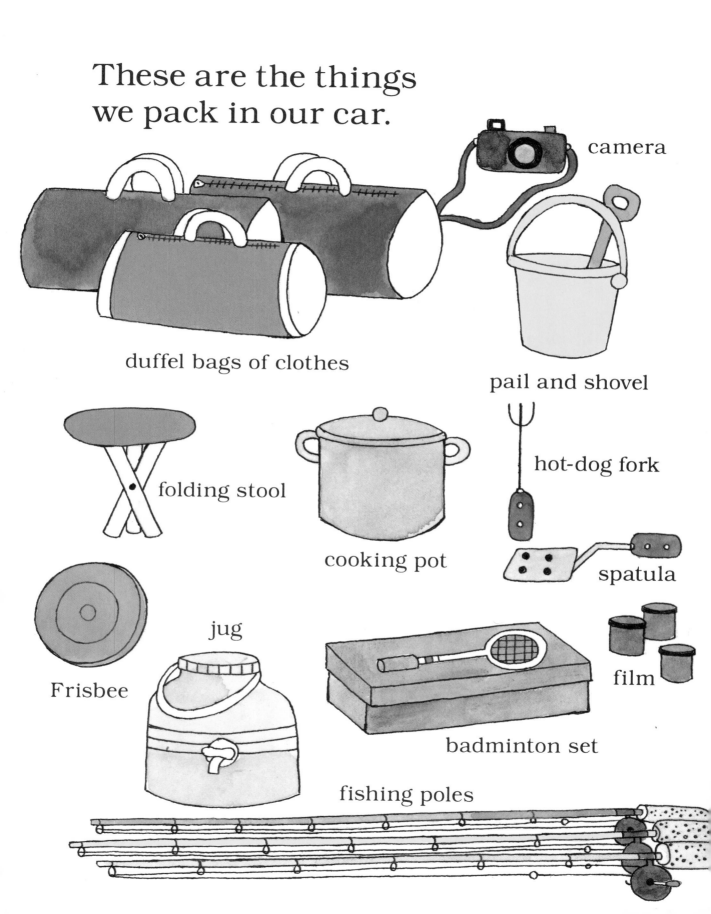

camera

duffel bags of clothes

pail and shovel

folding stool

cooking pot

hot-dog fork

spatula

Frisbee

jug

film

badminton set

fishing poles

fishing-tackle box

frying pan

my kite

canvas

easel

matches

charcoal

coffeepot

lantern

paints and brushes

sunscreen

binoculars

pen

sunglasses

books

air pump

We pack all these things too.

tote bags of towels, dishes
and odds and ends

cooler

surfboard

guitar

straw hat

bathing suits

address
book

cover-up

sleeping bags

scuffs

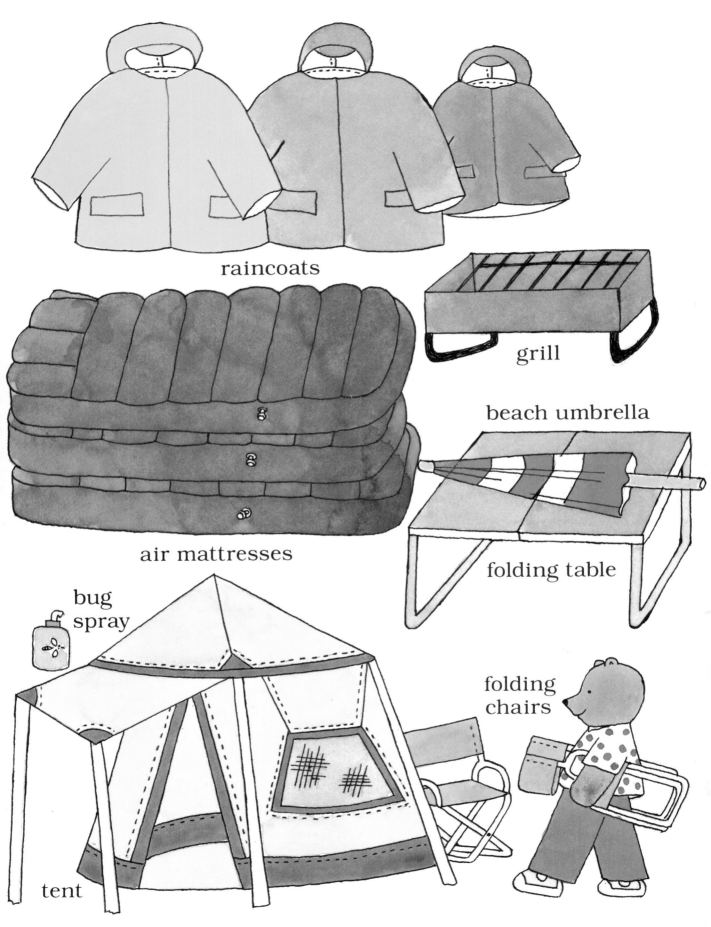

raincoats

grill

beach umbrella

air mattresses

folding table

bug spray

folding chairs

tent

We get in our car and away we go!

This is what we see as we drive along the road.

cars and trucks

EXIT 22 FERRYPORT

SLOW ROAD WORK

signs

STOP

road workers

hiker

farm stand

motorcyclist

picnic area

AR316

license plates

gas station

scarecrow

We drive to the ferry that will
take us to our vacation island.

Someone puts our car on the ferry.
We go up on deck as the boat sails away.

This is what we see from the deck of the boat.

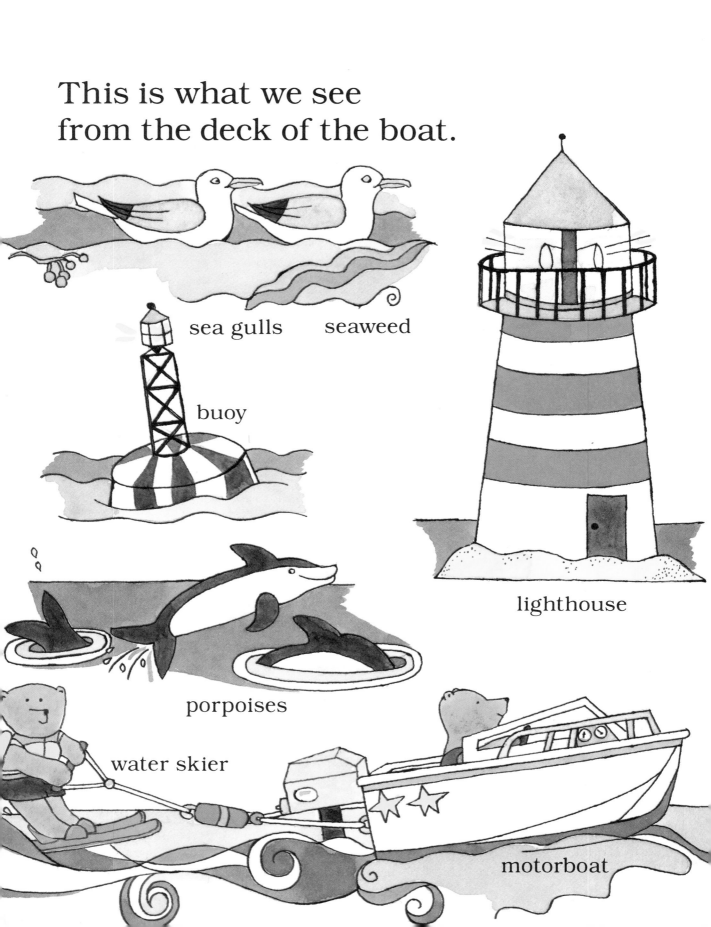

sea gulls

seaweed

buoy

lighthouse

porpoises

water skier

motorboat

tugboat and barge

fishing boat

sailboard

sailboat

jellyfish

rowboat

our island

When we get to our vacation island,
we find a good place to pitch our tent.

We will live in it for two weeks.

This is what we do after we have pitched our tent.

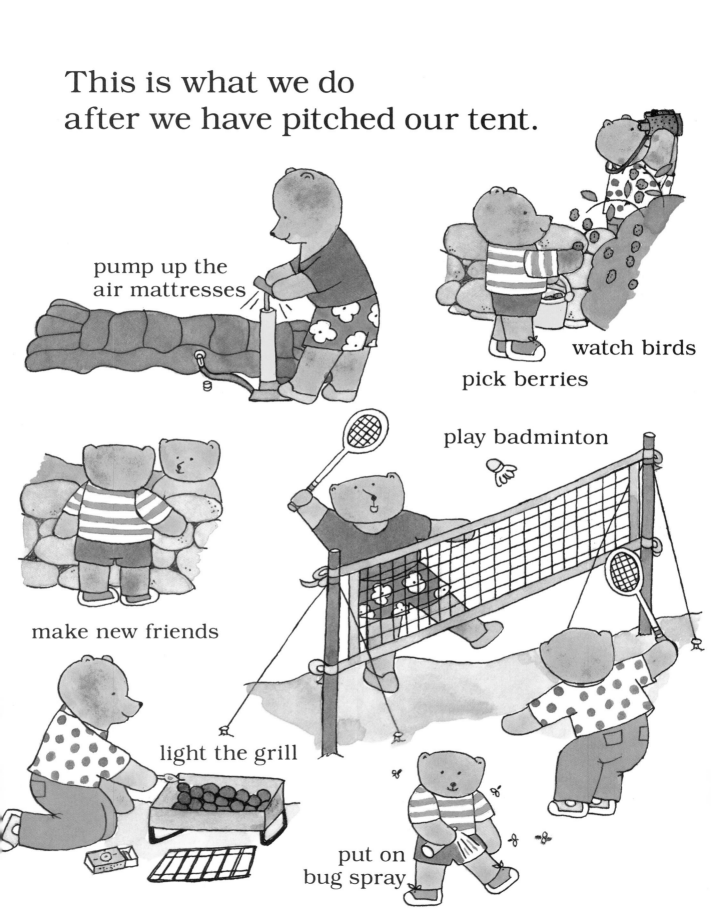

pump up the air mattresses

pick berries

watch birds

make new friends

play badminton

light the grill

put on bug spray

cook hot dogs

light the lantern

catch fireflies

throw out the garbage

play the guitar   sing songs

go to sleep

find the Big Dipper

In the morning, we go to the beach.

This is what we do at the beach.

play Frisbee

sunbathe

swim

dig holes to the ocean

fish

find seashells

build sand castles

take pictures   read

paint pictures

bury each other
in the sand

find
driftwood

fly kites

surf

drink lemonade

One day it rains,
so we cannot go to the beach.

This is what we do on the rainy day.

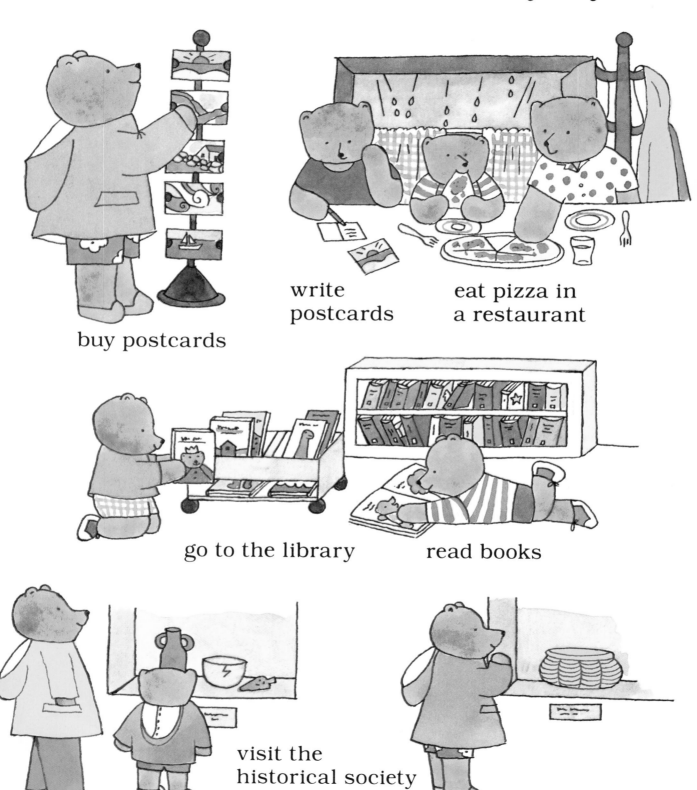

buy postcards

write
postcards

eat pizza in
a restaurant

go to the library

read books

visit the
historical society

tour the island

give someone a lift

buy gifts and souvenirs

sit on a hotel porch and drink lemonade

When two weeks have passed,
it is time to go home again.

We pack the car and say good-bye
to our island until next year.

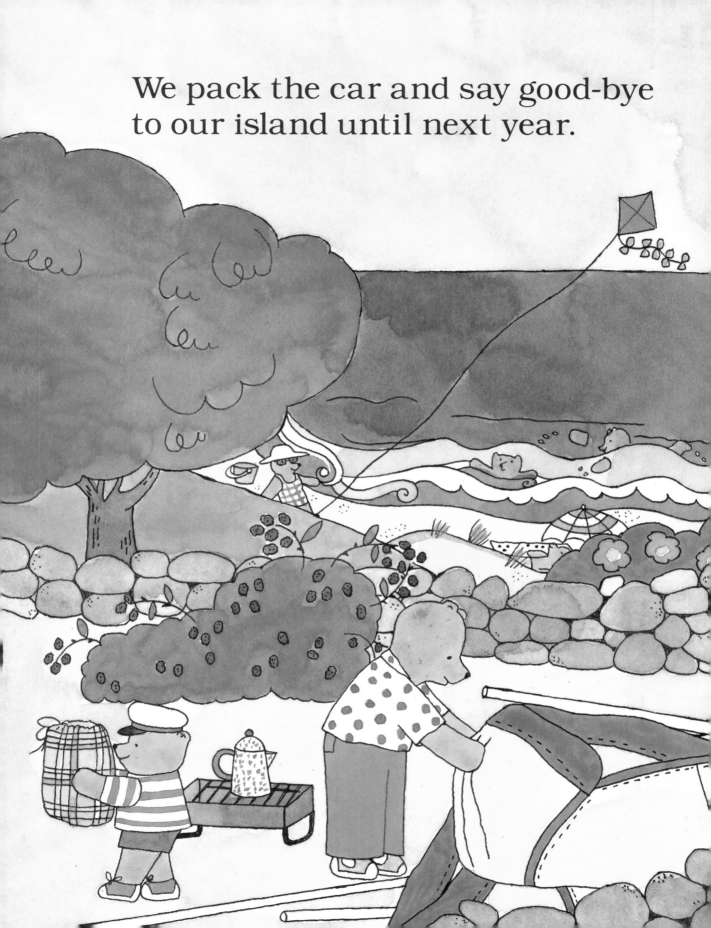

This is what we take home to remind us of our vacation.

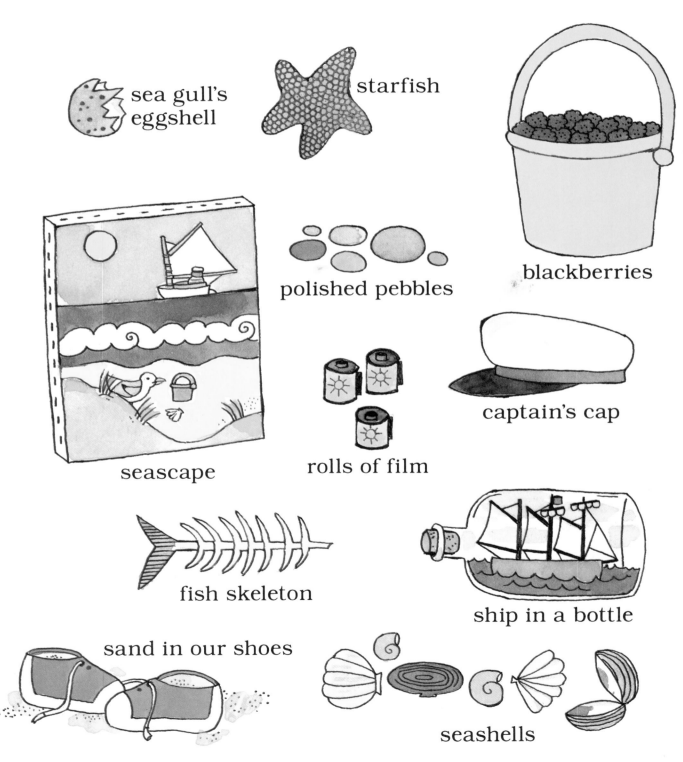

sea gull's eggshell

starfish

blackberries

polished pebbles

seascape

rolls of film

captain's cap

fish skeleton

ship in a bottle

sand in our shoes

seashells

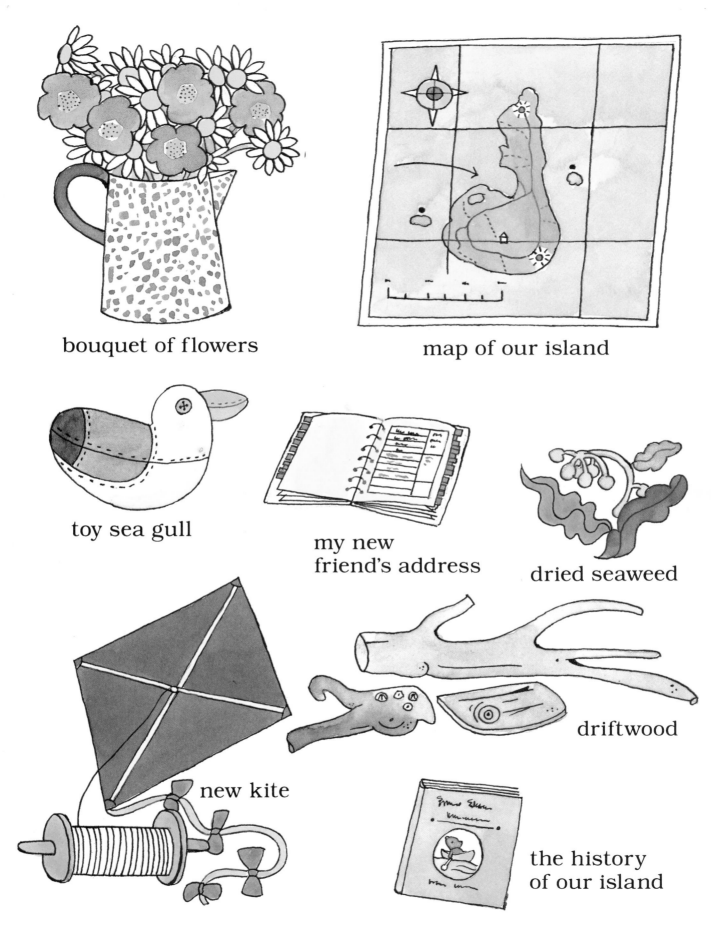

bouquet of flowers

map of our island

toy sea gull

my new
friend's address

dried seaweed

new kite

driftwood

the history
of our island

We ride on the ferry and drive home
in our car...just in time for supper.